The Lion of Soweto

And The Spelling Bee

Written by Zameer Dada
Inspired by a true story

Illustrations by Shayle Bester

AuthorHouse™ UK
1663 Liberty Drive
Bloomington, IN 47403   USA
www.authorhouse.co.uk
Phone: 0800 047 8203 (Domestic TFN)
+44 1908 723714 (International)

Because of the dynamic nature of the Internet, any web addresses or links contained in this book may have changed
since publication and may no longer be valid. The views expressed in this work are solely those of the author and do
not necessarily reflect the views of the publisher, and the publisher hereby disclaims any responsibility for them.

Any people depicted in stock imagery provided by Getty Images are models,
and such images are being used for illustrative purposes only.
Certain stock imagery © Getty Images.

This book is printed on acid-free paper.

ISBN: 978-1-7283-9577-7 (sc)
ISBN: 978-1-7283-9576-0 (e)

Print information available on the last page.

Published by AuthorHouse 11/22/2019

authorHOUSE®

The Lion Of Soweto

And The Spelling Bee

Written by Zameer Dada
Inspired by a true story
Illustrated by Shayle Bester

Education is the most powerful weapon
which you can use to change the world.

Nelson Mandela

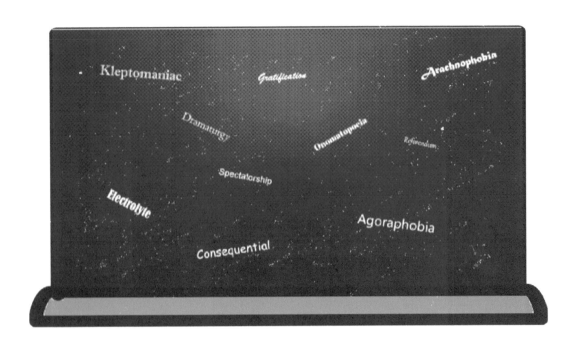

For my Family

Foreword

In the beginning was the spoken word. Five thousand years ago humans invented writing in the Middle East. With squiggles and wedges carved into stone and clay tablets, the spoken word was fleshed into letters. Spelling was born!

In the 1800's spelling bee contests started gaining momentum. First in the USA, then worldwide. For various reasons, the English language lends itself an excellent medium for spelling bee contests. Later, it spread to the world. Today, thousands of competitions are held all over the world bringing people of all ages, races and ideologies together. Language which originally divided people is now uniting them at local, national and international spelling bee contests.

One such contest is vividly described by Zameer Dada in this little story. He captures all the excitement, stress and fun in his story. These contests also stimulate the participants to learn new words and ideas further stimulating learning and reading. Students from all over the world exchange ideas about word origins promoting understanding of different cultures and knowledge of other countries.

I hope that these competitions might unite us all into one common community of nations and promote widespread world peace.

Dr Khalid Ismail

Foreword

Zameer Dada draws on his personal experience to create his first book which highlights the determination, commitment and sacrifices required to excel in any field, be it academic or sport and achieve one's goal.

Passion and a strong desire drive a young student from a challenging socio-economic background, Joseph Tau, to unleash his inner potential and ascend to great heights. His perseverance in reading leads to Joseph expanding his general knowledge and mastering new words with understanding, ultimately rewarding him handsomely.

In Joseph Tau, Zameer has created an appropriate and perfect role model which is so desperately required in the current South African context. We need more beacons of hope which the majority of South Africans can identify with and hope to be inspired by. Joseph's success symbolises what one can achieve through self-belief, ambition, resilience combined with appropriate mentorship and guidance from the community, leaders, parents and teachers.

"When you do things from your soul
You feel a river moving in you, a joy"
Rumi

Dr Ismail Dada

I would like to thank my parents Ashraf and Kuraysha for always encouraging me to do my best.

A huge thank you to Ntsako Mkhabela, founder of the Mzansi Spelling Bee, for introducing me to the Spelling Bee and motivating me to find my love for words. I would also like to thank Ntsako Mkhabela and the Nelson Mandela Children's Fund in assisting me with the launch of my book.

For their unconditional love, support and inspiration, I am forever indebted to my grandparents Ismail and Aysha Dada and Khalid and Khadija Ismail.

I am grateful for the great adventure and fantastic experiences I have with my siblings, Faeez, Yaseen, Naeem and Aliyah.

Zameer Dada

"Speller no 9!" calls out the Spelling Master. I get up from my seat and walk deliberately up to the microphone. My heart pounds with nervousness and excitement! If I get this word correct, I will be crowned the National Spelling Bee Champion! As I walk, I breath in deeply to calm my nerves.

How did I get here? This is my story...

My name is Joseph Tau. I am in Grade 8 at Ithemba School. I live in Diepkloof, Soweto with my younger sister and my parents. We live in a small, two-bedroom, beige house. My mum and dad are hard-working. They are always encouraging us to read and learn and do well at school. Every day, after school I have to do my homework before I can play with my friends. We play soccer on the streets pretending to be famous players. I want to be a striker like Beni McCarthy or Percy Tau (no, he is not my uncle).

Ms Khumalo, our English teacher walked into the class in February of last year and said: "Good Morning class, Grades 7 to 9 will be taking part in the National Spelling Bee. "What is that?", asked Thandi. Ms Khumalo explained that the spelling bee is like a spelling test in the form of a competition. She handed out a book with words and told us to learn them for the school spelling bee which was going to be a month later.

Many words were simple. I had come across them before. However, some words were long and complex and difficult to pronounce. I found them confusing. I promised myself I would try and do my best.

Every day after supper and after my homework, I would study the words. Many times, I had to do this under candle light. Electricity is very expensive, and we try and use the little electricity that we could afford for the essential things like the stove for cooking and heaters to keep warm.

I studied hard. My friend Thabo and I were very competitive. We decided that whoever made it to the next round would have the first pick of the best players amongst our friends for our soccer games, for the rest of the year.

The day of the first round of the spelling bee eventually came along. It was held in one of the larger classrooms. All the spellers were seated. The teachers sat in the front of the classroom. I sat patiently at the back awaiting my turn. I was one of the last spellers in my group. I watched my friends go to the front of the class. The teacher called out the word and one by one they spelt their words incorrectly and were knocked out of the competition. Just before my turn, a huge wave of nervousness flooded me. I thought, what if I, too, made a mistake? I didn't want to go out in the first round! As my name was called up, I took a deep breath and walked to the front of the class. My hands were sweaty. My heart was pounding against my chest. The teacher called out the word 'Burma'.

Nervously, I began spelling. "B – U – R – M – A, Burma."

There was a short applause after the teacher said, "That's correct."

"Wow," I thought, "that wasn't so bad." I took my seat again and awaited my next turn. I felt at ease.

The next few rounds flew by. I successfully went up three more times and spelt my words correctly. We were now down to the final 6 spellers.

The last 5 would advance to the provincial round. Thabo was called up before me. He spelled his word incorrectly. I felt his pain at being knocked out. A small part of me also felt some relief. All I had to do now, was spell my next word correctly. I would then advance to the next round and have the first pick of the best soccer players for our street soccer games.

My name was called out. Now I was anxious, thinking about soccer and the provincial round. "Your word is 'civilization'" uttered the teacher.

"C – I – V – I – L – I – Z – A – T – I – O – N, Civilization," I spelt.

"That is correct!" A huge cheer came from the audience and my friends. I made it through to the provincial round of the Spelling Bee.

Thabo high-fived me. Although we were competitive, we were close friends.

In the provincial round, I would be competing against children from across Gauteng. I remember thinking, "The provincial round will not be a walk in the park!" I consoled myself that making it to the provincial round was still a great achievement.

Every day after I completed my homework, I would go over the word list. There were very challenging words like, *hors d'oeuvres*, *pulchritude* and *ratatouille*. I just memorised these. I had a good memory.

I worked diligently every day. I took my spelling book wherever I went. I would wait outside my house for my taxi to school with my head buried in my book. During school breaks, while my friends played soccer, I would sit on the bench and keep at it. Sometimes, my friends would laugh and tease me, saying that I was wasting my time. "A boy from the townships will never be a spelling champion." Often, I too believed this, but I had to remind myself of a quote that our principal told us at assembly once, *"It is better to try and fail, than fail to try."*

The day of the provincial round arrived. Like I had anticipated, the provincial round was grander. There were children of all races from all corners of the province.

We were seated on the stage in a large school hall. Parents, guardians and supporters sat below the stage with eyes fixed on us. I felt the tension and pressure as I took a seat on the stage.

The Spelling Bee works as follows. Every speller is given a number. The spelling master calls out each speller by his or her number and then the word that must be spelt. The word checker writes down each letter called out by the speller keeping an accurate record. This makes it easy to check if the word is spelt correctly or not. The judge is a person who will decide what action to take if there is a problem, like someone challenging a spelling. After a word is called out, you can ask the spelling master for the meaning of the word, an example of how to use the word in a sentence, the origin of the word etc. Once you are ready, you can start spelling.

We started off with a practice round. Everyone had a chance to go up and spell and they would still be in regardless of whether they got it right or wrong. The practice round consisted of effortless words - words that any young junior high school child could spell. The idea was to boost everyone's confidence. I walked up and got the word 'though'.

"T – H – O – U – G – H, Though," I spelt confidently. There was applause from the audience. I found the applause supportive and uplifting. I believed I would be okay. This thought calmed me down.

Once the competition began, I was fortunate. I spelt my words correctly. Soon, we were down to the last 5. Only the top 3 in this round would qualify for the nationals. The nerves suddenly came rushing back. I was the first speller in the final round so I knew that if I spelt my word correctly, there was a good possibility that I would make it.

I walked up slowly, desperately trying to catch my breath. "Your word is palaeontologist" the spelling master said.

P - A - L - A - E - O - N - T - O - L - O - G - I - S - T

"P – A – L – A – E – O – N – T – O – L – O – G – I – S – T, Palaeontologist."

"That is correct." I fist bumped the air. I had the opportunity to make it to the national finals. Two more spellers dropped out in this round. So, it was a girl, another boy and I that progressed to the national finals. I was the only kid from a township school. I was representing Gauteng! Yay!

The National Spelling Bee final was held at the Johannesburg Theatre at the end of the year, after exams. I was excited. My mum and dad were there cheering me on. They were so proud. They told everyone of my achievement of reaching the finals of the National Spelling Bee. The National Spelling Bee final was the grandest of all the previous rounds.

It seemed I was a spelling whizz because before long, I found myself amongst the top three contestants. This was now the final stretch to glory or despair. I was the first speller of the final round. I walked slowly up to the microphone and tried to block out the rest of the world from my mind.

"Speller, your word is defamatory." "What is that?" I thought.

Me: "Can you please say the word again?"

Spelling Master: *"'dee-fam-mitry"*

I felt very uneasy. I had never heard this word.

I began spelling, "D – E – F – A – M – I – T – R – Y, Defamitry."

PING!

"I'm sorry, that is incorrect," the adjudicator uttered.

"The correct spelling is D – E – F – A – M – A – T – O – R – Y".

I knew this word. But I pronounced it as "*dee-fahm-ma-torie*". This was unfair!

I felt so cheated. How was I supposed to know that pronunciation if I had not heard it before? Our English in the township is heavily accented.

As I was lost in my thoughts, the next speller spelt her word correctly. She was eventually crowned the winner. My heart really sank when I heard that the first prize was a full scholarship to study a degree of her choice at Innovation University based in Johannesburg.

I had come third in the national finals. Yet I felt very sorry for myself. I thought I let my parents down. I was heartbroken.

That night, my parents told me how proud they were of me. Despite our difficult circumstances, I had done extremely well. My mum said that I could do better if I read more and studied hard. I would need to sacrifice my time playing soccer on the street.

I was determined there and then that I was going to win the next year's national finals of the National Spelling Bee. I was going to live up to my name and become the "Lion of Soweto". Tau means 'lion' in Tswana and Sotho. I promised myself that I would do everything needed to win.

The next day I went to the local library and registered for a library card. That holiday I spent more time reading than playing soccer. Thabo would come over. "Come umfana, let's play soccer." I would say, "I will play after I read this book".

I was enjoying reading. Not only did it open my eyes to a big wide world. I was learning about Greek mythology, science fiction, the empires of Mali and Mapungubwe. I didn't know that people of Mapungubwe built a wealthy empire (situated in the northern part of Limpopo) creating sophisticated trading routes with the Arabs and others. They sold gold and ivory and in return received glass and beads.

During my reading, I came across many new, complex words. I wrote each of these words down in a separate book. I looked up the meaning of these words. I wrote down a sentence using the word – often just using the sentence from the book I was reading. My vocabulary improved.

I would eventually go and play with the boys. After the game, we would sit around and talk. I would share with them the stories I was reading. I felt like an elder at whose feet we would sit at and listen to stories. My stories were different from my grandparents. My stories must have been very interesting. Thabo and a few others were encouraged to start reading. I was proud that I had a positive influence.

When school reopened, I went to my English teacher and asked for help with preparing for the spelling bee. I showed Ms Khumalo all the new words I mastered during my holidays. I asked her to assist me with the pronunciation used by first language English speakers. I was determined that our heavily accented township English was not going to be a problem for me.

Miss Khumalo guided me with pronunciation and she also helped me with learning about the origin of the words. Words with German origin tend to have 'tz', words with Greek origins have 'ph' instead of 'f'. My plan was to be fully prepared for the spelling bee. I was preparing for the spelling bee like a professional soccer player. I was determined to win this for me, my parents, my school, my friends and my township. I was determined to become a beacon of hope for all children.

Every night I stayed up late, working on mastering my words (my own personal list and from the official spelling bee list). I didn't let the studying by candle light slow me down.

I won my school competition easily. At the provincial round, I won easily without a stumble. My final word was Baccalaureate. Everybody was shocked that I knew the word baccalaureate.

As I prepared for the national finals, our afternoon soccer games were replaced by spelling training sessions. My friends would call out words and test me. My long walk home from school became spelling sessions with fellow learners walking to their homes in the same direction.

At home, my mum and dad tested me. At school, I practiced with my English teacher and class friends whenever we had a spare moment. Even the principal called me during one lunch break to help me. That was a very nerve-racking experience! Believe me!

I had the whole community behind me. Everybody supported me. They all wanted me to triumph. Have you heard the saying that it takes a village to bring up a child? Well, I had a whole village of supporters and spelling trainers backing me up.

The day of the National Spelling Bee final round creeped up a lot faster than expected.

The finals were in Soweto, my hometown! It was at the Soweto Theatre in Jabulani, which was about 10km away from my house.

We got to the theatre a good few hours before the competition. We were given instructions on how each province would walk in and where everyone should sit.

The time flew by and before I knew it, I was sitting on stage facing a theatre full of spectators.

Only a couple of minutes before I would walk up to the front of the stage to spell my word. *BA-DUM. BA-DUM. BA-DUM.* It felt like my heart was beating out of my chest. This was the ultimate stage. No room for error! Only one winner. My mind was focussed on winning that scholarship.

The rounds progressed slowly. I kept my cool and spelt my words correctly. I was now the last remaining speller.

"Speller no 9!" calls out the Spelling Master. I get up from my seat and walk deliberately up to the microphone. My heart pounds with nervousness and excitement! If I get this word correct, I will be crowned the National Spelling Bee Champion! As I walk, I breath in deeply to calm my nerves. It doesn't help! I am a bundle of adrenaline and nervousness!

"Speller, your word is, Ratatouille."

Me: "May I please have the origin of the word?"

Spelling Master: "French."

Me: "May I please have the definition?"

Spelling Master: "Vegetable dish of onions, tomatoes, aubergines and peppers fried and stewed in oil and sometimes served cold."

My heart races. I can barely breathe. I know this word!

"Ratatouille, R – A – T – A – T – O – U – I – L – L –, sorry may I please start over?" I ask. Eish! My nerves are getting the better of me.

"You may," the Spelling Master replies.

"R – A – T – A – T – O – U – I – L – L – E, Ratatouille," I spell.

"Congratulations speller, you are the National Spelling Bee Champion!"

"You have won a university scholarship from Innovation University!"

There is thunderous applause and a burst of cheers, screaming and chanting from the audience. "TAU! TAU! TAU!" There is no slowing down the adrenaline flowing through my body. I am experiencing the most natural high anyone could have! It is wonderful!

Against all odds, I beat the rest of the country and won the National Spelling Bee! It was a thrilling and exhilarating experience.

I discovered what hard work, discipline, a positive attitude and belief in myself can achieve for me.

I can picture tomorrow's newspaper headline: "Lion of Soweto rules The National Spelling Bee!"

Ntsako Mkhabela, the Founder and Director of the Mzansi Spelling Bee started the bee in 2012 as a response to the poor state of literacy in South Africa.

Mzansi Spelling bee is a national competition for children ages 9 to 16 or grades 4 to 10. Children from all over South Africa meet in community halls, class rooms, theatres and through stages of an interactive, challenging and fun game they compete to be crowned the Mzansi Speller of the year. At the heart of the Mzansi Spelling Bee is a desire to main stream literature and the love of words. If South Africa is serious about turning the tide on what is a literacy crisis every rule must be broken and ways found to reach out to the hearts and minds of not only South Africa's children but to every single parent, teacher, adult and citizen. In today's fast changing world we have very little to offer our children as tools for the future. The love of words and education is the only tool we can offer them to navigate a world that will be vastly different from our own. Through words we can raise confident children with the tools to dream, learn, create, break boundaries and explore the world.

We aim to contribute to the improvement of education and literacy in South Africa one word at a time, one child at a time.

Ntsako Mkhabela

Joseph's Word List

Burma: Myanmar (formally Burma) is a country in South East Asia

Civilization: The society, culture, and way of life of a particular area

Hors d'oeuvres: A small savoury dish, typically one served as an appetizer

Pulchritude: Beautiful

Ratatouille: Vegetable dish of onions, tomatoes, aubergines and pepper fried and stewed in oil and sometimes served cold

Diligently: In a way that shows care and conscientiousness in one's work or duties

Palaeontologist: A person who studies the branch of science concerned with fossil animals and plants

Defamatory: Damaging the good reputation of someone

Innovation: A new method, idea or product

Mythology: A set of stories or beliefs about a particular person, institution, or situation, especially when exaggerated or fictitious

Pronunciation: The way in which a word is said

Baccalaureate: A university bachelor's degree

ABOUT THE AUTHOR

Zameer Dada was the inaugural African Spelling Bee champion in 2016. Zameer was also a three time winner of the Mzansi Spelling Bee. He has advised The President's Award (TPA) for Youth Empowerment (associated with the Duke of Edinburgh's International Award) in arranging and co-adjudicating at their first TPA Spelling Bee in 2019. He is a Grade 11 learner at Sacred Heart College in Johannesburg. His school has exposed him to enriching, multiculturally diverse experiences which has contributed to him being comfortable in meaningfully connecting with others. Zameer is passionate about soccer, tennis, reading and speed cubing. Zameer lives in Johannesburg, South Africa with his parents Ashraf and Kuraysha, his brothers Faeez, Yaseen and Naeem and sister Aliyah.

Lightning Source UK Ltd.
Milton Keynes UK
UKHW050708021219
354499UK00010BA/52/P

ALL KINDS OF FAMILIES

FAMILIES WITH
TWO DADS

RACHAEL MORLOCK

PowerKiDS
press.

New York

Published in 2021 by The Rosen Publishing Group, Inc.
29 East 21st Street, New York, NY 10010

First Edition

Editor: Michelle Denton
Book Design: Reann Nye

Photo Credits: Cover kali9/iStock/Getty Images Plus/Getty Images; Series Art Vladislav Noseek/Shutterstock.com; pp. 5, 11 Africa Studio/Shutterstock.com; p. 7 FluxFactory/E+/Getty Images; p. 9 kate_sept2004/E+/Getty Images; p. 13 SolStock/E+/Getty Images; p. 15 PamelaJoeMcFarlane/E+/Getty Images; p. 17 Pixel-Shot/Shutterstock.com; p. 19 Michael Hanson/The Image Bank/Getty Images; p. 21 Kevin Wolf/ASSOCIATED PRESS.

Library of Congress Cataloging-in-Publication Data

Names: Morlock, Rachael, author.
Title: Families with two dads / Rachael Morlock.
Description: New York : PowerKids Press, 2020. | Series: All kinds of
    families | Includes index.
Identifiers: LCCN 2019050779 | ISBN 9781725317857 (paperback) | ISBN
    9781725317871 (library binding) | ISBN 9781725317864 (6 pack)
Subjects: LCSH: Same-sex parents. | Families.
Classification: LCC HQ75.27 .M67 2020 | DDC 306.874086/64-dc23
LC record available at https://lccn.loc.gov/2019050779

Manufactured in the United States of America

Some of the images in this book illustrate individuals who are models. The depictions do not imply actual situations or events.

CPSIA Compliance Information: Batch #CSPK20. For Further Information contact Rosen Publishing, New York, New York at 1-800-237-9932.

Find us on

CONTENTS

GROWING UP WITH TWO DADS

A family is a group of people, often related, who live together and care for one another. Many families are made up of parents—often a mom and dad—and their children.

But not all families are the same. Whether you have a mom and a dad, two moms, two dads, one parent, or another guardian, it's your love for each other that makes you a family. Today, more children than ever before are growing up in families with two dads.

In 2017, there were about 40,000 families with two dads in the United States.

5

BECOMING A FAMILY

Two men can marry or decide to spend their lives together. They can also choose to start a family. Gay fathers have different choices than families with a mom and a dad because they can't have a baby on their own. Instead, they often become fathers through adoption or other methods. It can be hard to start a family this way. If you have two fathers, they may have waited a long time to be able to share their home with you.

In 2004, Massachusetts became the first state to make a law saying that two men or two women could marry each other. Today, all 50 states have the same law.

7

FAMILIES THROUGH ADOPTION

Families with two dads often become families through adoption. Usually, an adopted child isn't **related** to their **adoptive parents**. They were born into a different family. They might even be from another country. When parents adopt a child, they promise to love them, keep them safe, and create a new family together.

In some families, an adopted child may know who their birth mother is. A birth mother is a woman who made an adoption plan and found a family to care for her baby.

Some children have been with their adoptive parents since the day they were born. Others are older and might be **fostered** by their adoptive parents first.

9

WHAT'S YOUR STORY?

Not all families with two dads are formed through adoption. Another option is called surrogacy. This is when a woman wants to help another family have a baby. She carries their baby in her **womb** until it's born. The dads adopt the baby together.

Children with two fathers might also have a second family with a mother. Every family is special. It's good to know the story about how your family came together.

You are an important part of your family's story. Your family came together because your parents wanted you in their lives.

11

LIFE WITH TWO DADS

Although kids join families with two dads in different ways, their everyday lives are like those of kids in other families. Children count on their parents to provide healthy food, help them learn and grow, offer a safe home, and give them love and attention. Two dads can do all these things. They can break up their tasks as parents based on their skills and what they like to do. As a team, two dads work together to make sure their family has what it needs.

Every family has their own **routine** for eating meals, spending time together, and taking part in school and other activities.

13

STANDING OUT

At certain times, families with two dads may stand out. Holidays like Mother's Day are reminders of how these families are different. Friends and strangers might also ask kids with two dads where their mother is.

Although they don't live with a mother, these kids have two parents who love and care for them. There are other important women in their lives too. Grandmothers, aunts, friends, and teachers can have a special part in **supporting** kids with two dads.

Fathers can be called by their first names or choose from nicknames such as Dad, Daddy, Papa, Pop, Papi, and other names. For example, one family might have a Daddy and a Papa.

GETTING CURIOUS

Kids from families with two dads may be curious about what it's like to live with a mom. Their friends probably wonder what it's like to have two dads. This curiosity is natural! Try talking with your friends about the ways your families are alike and different.

When you have these talks, show respect by listening carefully, being **polite**, and using kind words. You can learn a lot about your friends and their families when you show respect.

Talking about your differences can help you and your friends understand each other, but it can also be hard at times. You can choose how much of your story to share.

17

FEELING DIFFERENT

Many children feel sad, **embarrassed**, or angry about the things that make them seem different from others. Your feelings are real and important. It's good to talk and think about where they come from and how to deal with them.

If you have two dads, it's all right to ask questions about how your family is different. No two families are exactly the same. But what all strong families have in common is love and respect for one another.

You can be proud of your
family for who they are.

19

FEELING PROUD

Right now, families with two dads are less common than many other types of families. It took a long time before two men had the right to raise children together. Because of that, many people are still learning about families with two dads. They might have mistaken ideas about what families with two dads look and act like.

The best thing families with two dads can do is be themselves! When you are proud of who you are, others will be too.

Famous people like singer Ricky Martin (right) can help shine a light on families with two dads. Martin and his husband, Jwan Yosef, welcomed their fourth baby in 2019.

21

LOVE IS LOVE

If you have two dads, you probably know what it's like to be part of a loving family. You might also feel like your family is unusual. Everyone feels different and **uncomfortable** sometimes. Remembering those feelings can help you be kind, respectful, and welcoming to other people of different **backgrounds**.

The story of how you became a family is an important part of who you are. Even more important are the everyday ways you work together to love and care for each other.

GLOSSARY

adoptive parent: A parent who has adopted a child.

background: All of a person's experiences, knowledge, and situation.

embarrassed: Feeling upset, ashamed, or uneasy.

foster: To give parental care to a child who isn't adopted or related.

polite: Showing courtesy or good manners.

related: Having a connection by blood.

routine: A regular way of doing things in a particular order.

support: To provide help and guidance.

uncomfortable: A feeling of uneasiness.

womb: The part of the body that grows a baby.

INDEX

WEBSITES

Due to the changing nature of Internet links, PowerKids Press has developed an online list of websites related to the subject of this book. This site is updated regularly. Please use this link to access the list: www.powerkidslinks.com/akof/dads